PUFFIN B

Praise for *The Legend of Spud Murphy* and
The Legend of Captain Crow's Teeth:

'The funniest book of the year. A mini-masterpiece'
– *Daily Mail*

'A treat. This tale shines thanks to deft story-telling and laugh-out-loud bits' – *Funday Times*

'Guaranteed to convert the most book-resistant boy'
– *Sunday Telegraph*

'Hilarious' – *Scotsman*

'Family capers and plenty of full-on belly laughs'
– *Sunday Times*

'This story is great fun – readers are in for a most enjoyable romp' – *Books for Keeps*

'A wonderfully entertaining adventure' – *Scottish Daily Mail*

'Cracking' – *Disney's Big Time*

Books by Eoin Colfer

THE LEGEND OF SPUD MURPHY
THE LEGEND OF CAPTAIN CROW'S TEETH
THE LEGEND OF THE WORST BOY IN THE WORLD

And for older readers

ARTEMIS FOWL
ARTEMIS FOWL: THE GRAPHIC NOVEL
ARTEMIS FOWL AND THE ARCTIC INCIDENT
ARTEMIS FOWL AND THE ETERNITY CODE
ARTEMIS FOWL AND THE OPAL DECEPTION
ARTEMIS FOWL AND THE LOST COLONY

AIRMAN

HALF MOON INVESTIGATIONS

THE SUPERNATURALIST

THE WISH LIST

EOIN COLFER

The Legend of THE WORST BOY IN THE WORLD

Illustrated by Tony Ross

PUFFIN

PUFFIN BOOKS

Published by the Penguin Group
Penguin Books Ltd, 80 Strand, London WC2R 0RL, England
Penguin Group (USA) Inc., 375 Hudson Street, New York, New York 10014, USA
Penguin Group (Canada), 90 Eglinton Avenue East, Suite 700, Toronto, Ontario, Canada M4P 2Y3
(a division of Pearson Penguin Canada Inc.)
Penguin Ireland, 25 St Stephen's Green, Dublin 2, Ireland (a division of Penguin Books Ltd)
Penguin Group (Australia), 250 Camberwell Road, Camberwell, Victoria 3124, Australia
(a division of Pearson Australia Group Pty Ltd)
Penguin Books India Pvt Ltd, 11 Community Centre, Panchsheel Park, New Delhi – 110 017, India
Penguin Group (NZ), 67 Apollo Drive, Rosedale, North Shore 0632, New Zealand
(a division of Pearson New Zealand Ltd)
Penguin Books (South Africa) (Pty) Ltd, 24 Sturdee Avenue, Rosebank, Johannesburg 2196, South Africa

Penguin Books Ltd, Registered Offices: 80 Strand, London WC2R 0RL, England

puffinbooks.com

First published 2007
This edition published 2008
1

Set in Baskerville MT
Made and printed in England by Clays Ltd, St Ives plc

British Library Cataloguing in Publication Data
A CIP catalogue record for this book is available from the British Library

ISBN: 978-0-141-31893-6

For Finn and Seán,

the best boys in the world

contents

CHAPTER 1

It's Not Fair

I have four brothers, and they are always complaining about something. If I ever have a problem, and I go to my mum to talk about it, there are generally at least two brothers in the queue before me, moaning about something totally stupid. I could have an actual real problem like a hangnail or a missing sock, and there they are wasting Mum's time with silly stuff like jam on their faces or back-to-front jumpers.

My four brothers have their favourite

problems that they like to moan about at least once a day. Mum calls these problems their *hobby horses*. Whenever they start whinging on about them, Dad makes horsey noises and a here-we-go-again face, but Mum listens anyway because she's our mum.

Marty is the oldest brother, and his hobby horse is that he's never allowed do anything, and he might as well be in prison.

'Why can't I have a motorbike?' he often whines. 'I'm ten now and that's nearly sixteen. If I had a helmet on, the police would never notice.'

Or another one is: 'Why can't I have a full-sized snooker table in the garage? It's only full of old tools and a car, nothing important. I'll pay for the snooker table as soon as I become a famous football player.'

Dad sometimes comes into a room just to hear Marty complain about something. He says that Marty is far more entertaining than any television show.

'Snooker table,' Dad chuckles. 'Marty, my boy. You are cracking me up.'

This is not what Marty wants to hear, so he storms off sulking. Once when Marty came back after storming off, Dad presented him with a cardboard Oscar for best actor.

My name is Will and I'm the next in line.

After me comes my second brother, Donnie, whose hobby horse is his hair. No matter how often Mum washes or combs it, there's always something wrong.

'It's sticking up at the back, Mum.' So Mum flattens the back.

'Now, Donnie, off you go.'

'It's still sticking up, Mum.'

'No, it isn't. You're having hair hallucinations, Donnie. Go on now, you'll be late for school.'

'I can see a hair sticking up. It's definitely there. The girls will see, and I'll get a nickname. Sticky-Up Woodman they'll call me. It'll be horrible.'

And so Mum gets out a water bottle and sprays Donnie's head.

'Better?'

'I suppose.'

This happens every second day. On the

other days, Donnie wants his hair to stick up, because he thinks it's cool.

Brothers three and four, Bert and HP, have invented brand-new words so that they can whinge more efficiently. Bert's new word is 'canniva', as in: 'Canniva bar of chocolate?'

'Not before your dinner, honey,' says Mum.

'Canniva square, just one square.'

'No, honey. Dinner's on the way.'

'Canniva bag of crisps then?'

'I think you're missing the point, Bert. No sweets or crisps before your dinner.'

'Canniva throat sweet?'

'Throat sweets are still sweets, honey.'

Mum has great patience. Dad only puts up with two 'cannivas' before he gets annoyed.

HP (Half Pint) is the youngest and hates being the baby. The word he invented to complain about this is 'snoffair', as in: 'Snoffair. Chrissy's mummy allowed him to get his head shaved, now he looks at least five and a half.' He said this one afternoon after his half-day in baby infants.

'I'm not in charge of Chrissy,' said Mum. 'I'm only in charge of you. And I say, no head shaving.'

'Snoffair,' howled HP. 'Barry has a stick-on tattoo, like the big boys.'

'No stick-on tattoo. We've talked about this.'

'Snoffair,' muttered HP, then: 'What about

an earring then? Loads of people have those. Snoffair that I don't have one.'

'Life's not fair sometimes,' said Mum, and hugs HP until he starts sucking his thumb. Two minutes later he is fast asleep.

Sometimes HP talks in his sleep. Guess what he says . . .

All this complaining means that by the time Marty and I get home from school with our troubles there is usually a little brother perched on each of Mum's knees, moaning about their baby problems. And even if, miracle of miracles, there is a free knee, Mum is usually on auto-nod by then anyway. Auto-nod is when grown-ups don't really listen to what a child says; they just nod every five seconds or so until the child goes away.

So Marty and I decided that we had to target another grown-up to talk to about our problems. Dad was the next target, but sometimes he works so late that we don't even see him before bedtime. Marty reckoned that Dad only had time for one set of complaints, and that set should be his. So I had to pick someone else. Somebody who was a good listener and had a lot of spare time. I knew just the person.

Grandad.

Chapter 2
Grandad

Every weekend, Dad loads us all into the car and we drive thirty miles down the coast to *his* mum and dad's home. Our grandparents live in the seaside village of Duncade, which is on a headland that sticks out into the sea like a Stone Age arrowhead.

Grandad is one of the two Duncade lighthouse keepers and he lives with our gran in an apartment on the ground floor. When I grow up, I plan to take over Grandad's job and live in the lighthouse apartment. I will hang a

sign on the door that says NO LITTLE BROTHERS ALLOWED. There won't be any girls allowed either, except my mum who can come in to make dinners and do washing and stuff.

Grandad has already started training me for the job. Every Saturday we climb the 116 steps to the very top of the lighthouse to polish the lighthouse lenses in the lamp room. Grandad wears a special canvas belt with pockets for polishing cream, rags and a water bottle. For my ninth birthday Grandad made a belt for me too.

'I learned to stitch in the merchant navy,' he explained that day, buckling the belt around my waist. 'Now you are my official helper.'

I like being Grandad's official helper because it is something just for me. Marty won't help because there is no money involved, and my little brothers are not allowed to climb the narrow spiral staircase because it's too dangerous.

So Grandad and I climb the steps together. I count every one just in case some have gone missing. But the number is always the same – 116 – if you count the giant first step twice.

'That's Peg Leg Byrne's giant step,' Grandad told me once. 'All the steps used to be that big, until Peg Leg Byrne, a lighthouse keeper with a wooden leg, chiselled them all down, starting at the top. It took him thirty years, and unfortunately he died before he could do the last one. All that because the steps were a little high for him.'

It seems as though each step has a story, and sometimes Grandad tells me them all before we reach the top. But finally we make it, and the first thing we do is take a long drink from our water bottles. Not too long though, because there are 116 steps between us and the nearest bathroom.

The lamp room has glass all the way round, so that the light can get out. This means that anyone in the lamp room has a fantastic view of the sea and the headland. In front of us, lines of white waves roll in from the horizon, and behind us the headland cuts a grey line through the sea.

'People in America would pay big money for a view like this,' says Grandad. He says this every single time, and he is probably right.

After a moment admiring the view, we climb up an old wooden ladder into the lamp itself. This is like climbing inside a giant glass vase, and when you are in there you get an idea of how the world must look to a goldfish. The lenses magnify everything until even a fly sitting on the glass looks like a giant bug-eyed monster.

One Saturday while we were inside the lenses, I told Grandad about my problem.

'I have a problem, Grandad,' I said, pouring some polish on to my favourite rag.

'What would that be, Bosun?'

Grandad calls me Bosun, which means

second in command.

'My problem is . . . problems. I have no one to tell my problems to. Mum and Dad are always too busy.'

'That *is* a problem,' said Grandad, spreading a blob of polish across one of the lenses. 'Everybody needs someone to talk to.'

'So, I thought, maybe you could be my someone. Gran says that you don't do much except polish the lenses.'

'Oh really? Is that what your gran says?'

'Yes. She says the lighthouse computer does all the work, and you just hang around up here pretending to be busy.'

'I see. So you reckon I would have plenty of time to listen to your problems?'

'I reckon so.'

Grandad stopped polishing. 'OK, Bosun, I'll make you a deal. I'll listen to your sob stories, if you listen to mine.'

This sounded fair to me, so I stuck out my hand.

'It's a deal.'

Grandad shook my hand. 'Just one story a week though. I don't want to be crying myself to sleep every Saturday night.'

'One story a week.'

'And if they're only small problems, exaggerate a bit, just to keep things interesting. I like stuff with jungle animals.'

'OK, Grandad,' I said, although none of

my complaints had anything to do with jungle animals. There was a cat next door that always hissed at me, but that probably didn't count.

Grandad finished polishing, and stuffed the rag back into his belt.

'Right then. Round one next Saturday. I hope something really bad happens to you, because I have stories that I've wanted to get off my chest for years.'

And, funny as it seems, I kind of hoped something bad would happen to me too. Something with jungle animals.

Chapter 3
Tinfoil

I could not wait to get down to Duncade the next weekend. I was bursting to tell Grandad what had happened to me in school. Even as it was happening, I was thinking that it would make a great story for Grandad. The only thing missing was a gorilla, or maybe a screeching monkey.

Grandad would not let me start until we had started polishing the lenses.

'OK, Bosun,' he said then. 'Let's hear it. Your face is red from trying to hold it in.'

'It's so embarrassing,' I said, scrubbing a large circle in the dusty lens. 'There's no way you're going to beat this.'

'We'll see, Bosun. We'll see.'

And so I told Grandad the story of that week's problem.

'Nothing much happened all week, and I thought I would have nothing to tell you. Then Thursday came along.'

'As it often does,' said Grandad.

'So there I was. In class. Being a brilliant student, as usual.'

'What a nightmare,' said Grandad.

'No. That's not it. The embarrassing bit happened about two o'clock. When I had to ask our teacher – our *female* teacher – if I could go to the bathroom.'

Grandad stopped polishing. 'Is that it? Tell me there's more.'

'Yes, there's more. I went into the toilet and

there was no paper. But I didn't notice this until after I had been. If you know what I mean.'

'Oh,' said Grandad. 'This could be nasty.'

'So I had to shout to the teacher to bring some in,' I said, covering my face with my hands. 'Everybody heard. I was super embarrassed. It was terrible. You have no idea.'

ICK

It felt good, sharing my story with Grandad. Just talking about it made the memory less embarrassing.

Grandad snorted. 'That's nothing. You want an embarrassing toilet story, listen to this. When *I* was young, we couldn't afford toilet paper. So my mother used whatever was lying around. First we used newspaper, then crisp bags, then bits of cardboard boxes. Once I even had to use tinfoil.'

'Tinfoil?'

Grandad nodded sadly. 'Yep. My bottom was magnetized for a week. Everywhere I went, compasses and drawing pins followed me. I learned to check before sitting down.'

'Wow,' I said.

'Yep,' said Grandad. 'Now that's an embarrassing toilet story. Are you sure you want to go on with this swapping complaints thing? Because, to be honest, I was nearly nodding off during your story.'

'Yes, I want to keep swapping stories. I'm sure something really terrible will happen to me next week.'

Unfortunately, the worst thing that happened the following week was that I lost my pencil. When I told Grandad about this, he responded with a tale about having his entire schoolbag stolen by a badger who had mistaken it for another badger.

The week after that I was certain that I would win. The barber had slipped when he was trimming the back of my head with electric clippers and had shaved a bald strip right up to my crown. Grandad took a long look at the bald strip, then took off his flat cap and showed me where a shark had bitten him on the head.

'That's a good one,' I admitted, then asked if I could borrow his cap.

It was no use. Whatever happened to me, something a million times worse had happened to Grandad. He just reached into the past and pulled out these brilliant stories. I had no chance. He was seventy and I was only nine, so he had a lot more memories to choose from. Anyway, nothing really terrible had ever happened to me. Nothing that could compare with a shark bite on the head. Or if something

had happened, it must have been when I was really young. Something that I couldn't remember.

I would have to ask Dad, I decided. He would remember if something horrible had ever happened to me as a baby. Something that even Grandad couldn't top.

Chapter 4
Jelly Baby

I managed to get Dad on his own the following Wednesday. Generally Marty would latch on to our father as soon as he walked in the door, but, as luck would have it, Marty had an abscess on his tooth and was upstairs in bed.

I waited until Dad had put away his carpenter's belt, and was at the kitchen table with a cup of tea before nabbing him.

'Dad, I need to ask you something.'

'Have you cleared it with Marty?' joked Dad.

'Marty can't talk today. Whenever he opens his mouth, the cold air hurts his abscess.'

'OK, good. I mean bad. It's bad that poor Marty is sore, but it's good that we can talk. So, what do you want to talk about, Will?'

I climbed up on a chair. 'Me and Grandad are having a sort of competition. Every Saturday, I tell him about my main problem of the week, and then he tells me one of his from ages ago.'

'That sounds great,' said Dad. 'It's good to have someone to talk to. And you *are* the Bosun, so who better than your grandad?'

'That's what I thought, but . . .'

'But what?'

'But Grandad's stories are so much better than mine. He has sharks and badgers and tinfoil. All I have are clippers and toilet paper.'

Dad nodded seriously. 'Sharks are better than clippers.'

'I can't remember one terrible thing ever happening to me. Not one.'

Dad scratched the stubble on his chin. 'Well, there was *one* thing. You were only two at the time, so you probably don't remember it.'

My eyes opened wide. 'Was it terrible?'

'Oh yes.'

'And dangerous?'

'Absolutely.'

'Tell me, Dad. And don't leave out any

details. I need the dangerous, terrible truth.'

So Dad told me this story. It was dangerous and it was terrible, but, best of all, it was true.

Seven years ago, there were only three brothers in the Woodman house as Bert and HP hadn't been born yet. Donnie was still a baby who spent most of his time getting his nappy changed and trying to escape from the playpen. Only Marty and I were free to roam around the house. I don't remember any of this; I'm just taking Dad's word for it. But one thing I do remember, even after seven years, is the weekly jelly baby.

Every Friday, Gran drove in from Duncade to visit her grandsons. When she came through the front door, Gran always sang the first line of a made-up song.

'Who's the best boy in the world?' she sang, dancing a little jig. And whoever could finish

the song with the words 'I am' would get a special prize. A red jumbo jelly baby, big enough to suck on for an entire afternoon.

Marty had always claimed the precious prize because he was the only one able to talk. He began speaking at the age of one and a half, whereas I didn't say much until I was nearly three. Gran had normal-sized jelly babies for the rest of us to suck on, but we were all jealous of the red jumbo, even Donnie, who just mashed any sweets he got into his hair, then wondered why bees were following him around.

Marty was very proud of his jumbo jelly baby. It was one of the things that marked him out as leader of the pack. Every Friday, after he had the jelly baby safely in his hand, he would seek me out and play a mean little game.

'What's this?' he would ask, holding up the jelly baby.

'A baby,' I would snivel, knowing what was coming.

'And what is Will?' was always Marty's second question.

'Will baby,' I would answer, knowing this was what Marty wanted to hear.

'Then this must be you,' Marty would conclude and viciously bite off the jelly baby's head.

'Blaaaaah,' I would blubber in shock. If Marty was in an especially mean mood, he would squeeze the jelly baby's body, until red jelly oozed from the neck hole.

'That's your guts,' he would declare, at which point the two-year-old version of me would run squealing to Mum and tell on Marty.

Unfortunately I only knew about thirty words at that point, so all I could say to Mum was, 'Marty ate jelly baby.'

Which doesn't sound that serious, does it?

This went on for ages. And as long as Marty got the jumbo and the rest of us got normal-sized jelly babies, our big brother was happy. But every Friday I longed to be the one who could finish Gran's song and claim the jumbo before Marty could tease me with it.

My chance came one Friday morning when Gran arrived early. Marty was in the kitchen when the front door opened. Donnie was in the playpen and I was positioned perfectly in the front hall.

Gran came in singing. 'Who's the best boy in the world?' she sang.

I was so excited that I couldn't say the words. 'Myemam,' I blurted.

Gran tickled my chin. 'Did you say something, little Will?'

I closed my eyes, took a deep breath and said clearly, 'I . . . am.'

'Well,' said Mum who was passing through

on her way to the kitchen. 'It looks like you will have to bring two jumbo jelly babies with you in future. We have another big boy here now.'

And so Gran took a tissue from her handbag, and unwrapped the jelly baby inside it. It lay on her palm, red and juicy and perfect. I took it carefully, as though it were the most precious jewel in a pirate's collection.

The jumbo was mine.

I licked it once, to make sure it was real, then jammed the whole thing into my mouth, in case a certain someone tried to steal it.

Marty came out of the kitchen just in time to see a big, fat, red dribble roll down over my chin. For a moment he didn't know what was going on, then he saw Gran and the empty tissue in her hand.

'My jumbo,' he said. 'But I'm the big boy.'

I was expecting fireworks. When Marty lost his temper, it could be really spectacular. But

there were no fireworks that day. Marty simply turned and walked out of the room without another word.

If I had known what was coming, I think I might have preferred some fireworks.

CHAPTER 5

Up the Jumper

When Marty saw me sucking on the jumbo jelly baby, he made a decision. This decision was that there wasn't enough room in the house for two jumbo-jelly-baby eaters. One of us had to go, and it wasn't going to be him. Marty decided that it would be better if I went off to live somewhere else, but the trick was how to get me to leave. He knew that I was quite fond of Mum and Dad, and that I might not like the idea of moving out.

Marty thought about this for a while. He was a big fan of nature programmes, so he decided the best way to find out how to make me leave was to watch me the way birdwatchers watch birds. Marty built himself a little tent behind the sofa with a blanket and three pillows, then crawled in with some supplies to spy on his baby brother. My gran thought this was hilarious and extremely cute, but she didn't know what was really going on.

Marty stayed in that tent for at least twenty minutes, which was the longest he had ever stayed in one spot. Even in bed Marty shifted about as though he was plugged in. Marty often went to sleep in one bed and woke up in another.

In those twenty minutes, my big brother discovered three things about me. One, I dribbled a lot. Two, I wasn't potty-trained yet and had to get my nappy changed quite often, and three, I loved to walk on straight lines. This last thing is something I still do. Whenever I see a straight line on the path, road or carpet, I like to walk along it and pretend I am a circus tightrope-walker. I am never happier than when I am walking on a straight line.

Marty thought about the straight-line walking for a while, and came up with an idea.

If he could find a really long straight line for me to walk on, then I would leave home and walk along the straight line until I came to a new house to live in. This doesn't sound like a particularly brilliant plan, but for a little kid it's not bad.

As it happened, Marty knew exactly where to find such a straight line, but it was somewhere we were forbidden to go. Somewhere extremely dangerous that Marty had seen from the car. He decided that it was worth any risk, for a weekly supply of jumbo jelly babies.

Marty waited until Mum and Gran were in the kitchen, then he crawled out of his tent and across to where I was dancing to the music in my head, the way two-year-olds do.

'Hey, Will,' he said, knocking on my forehead to see if there was anyone in there. 'Wanna play a game?'

I rubbed my head, but I wasn't upset. Marty knocked on my head so often that I thought this was how kids said hello to each other.

'Play game,' I said, nodding. Marty hardly ever offered to play with me. In fact he viewed playing with his little brothers as punishment, and would beg to be sent to bed instead.

'OK,' said Marty. 'Let's play walking the line.'

'Walking the line,' I agreed.

Marty put a finger to his lips. 'This is a secret game. No telling Mum.'

I put a finger to my own lips and blew a wet raspberry.

'Secret game,' I said, attempting a wink. When I was very young, winking and whistling were the two things I thought I could do, but I couldn't. What I was really doing was blinking and humming.

Marty wiped the raspberry dribble from his face with my left ear. Not my actual ear, the ear of the blue bunny jumpsuit I was wearing. I can still remember that bunny jumpsuit. I wore it until I was four, even though it was for age twelve to eighteen months. Eventually Mum had to cut the feet off it so I could squeeze myself in. I loved that bunny suit, especially the woolly hood that protected my ears from the wind, and the two bunny ears that flopped when I ran. It was like an all-over security blanket. Marty used those ears to wipe up anything he spilled, and was forever grabbing my head and dragging me off to mop up stuff.

'I know where the biggest, best straight line in the world is. Wanna see?'

My eyes were wide. 'Yes, please.' I have always had excellent manners.

'OK. Then you have to go up the jumper.'

Up the Jumper was a game we often played, when Marty could be bothered to play with either of his smaller brothers. It was an easy game to learn. You simply stuffed yourself up Marty's jumper, wiggled your head and arms through the holes, and then waddled around the house screaming like a two-headed, four-armed monster. Mum and Dad always enjoyed watching us play Up the Jumper, unless Marty was wearing his good jumper.

What I didn't know was that when we were playing Up the Jumper, the second person in the jumper was hidden from anyone behind. Gran and Mum could only see Marty now, and must have thought that I had climbed into the playpen with Donnie.

Marty knocked on the back of my head, and because my arm was in his sleeve, I knocked on my head too.

'Stand on my feet,' he ordered.

'Feet, Mary,' I agreed and put my blue boots on his trainers. I was not always able to pronounce Marty properly when I was two, so I often called him Mary, which he didn't like very much.

'Marty! Mar-tee! Yes, walking the line. We have to go through the gates.'

I was horrified. 'Gates?'

'Yes. Through the gates. Now are you

coming or not?'

'Coming.' I said. Even though we were not allowed through the gates, I didn't want to miss out on the best straight line in the world.

'Good. Well, shush then. This is supposed to be a secret game.'

I shushed. Everyone knew that secret games were the best ones. Even a two-year-old knew that.

So Marty walked out the back door, into our yard. From there he went around the side and used a stick to open the safety gate. Five years later, HP would use that same stick to open the gate. It was a sturdy stick.

Once he had the safety gate open, Marty pulled up his jumper and I spilled out.

'OK, blue bunny,' he said. 'Run after Marty.'

'Run after Mary,' I said, climbing to my feet. I was getting quite excited. The best straight line in the world was nearby. In my two-year-old brain, I imagined a glowing white line in the sky. It tied itself up like a shoelace, but instead of a double bow, it had a face.

'Hurry,' said Marty, aware that Mum might discover our jailbreak any second.

I trotted after Marty, bunny ears jiggling, down the drive to the front gate. This was the edge of my daily world. I had never been past the front gate without a grown-up.

'Gate,' I said nervously.

'Gate,' agreed Marty, wrapping both hands around the sprung catch. He swung on that catch like a monkey, until his weight dragged it down. This was a valuable skill indeed. Who knows how long Marty had been escaping to the outside world this way.

The gate swung open, and it seemed to me that the noise from outside suddenly got a lot louder.

'Mummy,' I said, lip quivering.

Marty knew he was on the verge of losing me and had to think fast.

'Look!' he shouted, pointing. 'The line!'

'Line!' I squeaked in delight, and followed Marty through the gateway, into the forbidden zone.

Our house was in a brand-new estate, in the middle of a brand-new part of town. All around us were mini-mountains of sand and giant cubes of blocks.

We ignored shiny new playground swings and roundabouts, heading straight for the mysterious and wonderful line. All the way across the grass, the imaginary line in my head was calling me on.

Faster, faster. I'm waiting for you.

Soon we came to the edge of the estate. This was new territory for me. The only thing separating us from the rest of the world was a steel fence, and, looking back, I can see how someone like Marty was never going to be

beaten by a mere steel fence.

Sure enough, my big brother found a spot where we could wriggle underneath.

'Dogs go this way,' he explained, pulling me through by the bunny ears. He was right. My bunny jumpsuit smelled like dog. Now Mum would have to wash it again, and I would hang around by the dryer until it was ready to wear.

We were now at the side of a huge road. Roads were the most forbidden places in the world – places where speeding cars and giant trucks roared past, with grilles like dinosaur teeth, ready to gobble up any little boys silly enough to put a toe on the tarmacadam.

'Road,' I said, in a wobbly, worried voice.

'This is a special road,' said Marty. 'Look! No cars!'

Marty was right. There were no cars. Not a single one. To prove this point, he danced out into the middle of the black road, waving his arms and screeching like a monkey, daring the cars to come and get him.

I know now that there were no cars because the road was not finished. It was part of the new highway that would connect our town to Dublin.

Marty pointed at the ground. 'Here's the line. Look!'

My eyes followed his finger. There, running down the middle of the road, was the most beautiful white line I had ever seen. It was fat and speckled with sparkles, and I was immediately under its spell.

Walk along me, Will, said the line. *Walk along me forever.*

And the line did seem to go on forever, stretching off into the distance.

'You walk along the line,' said Marty, urging me on with a little tug on my left ear.

I tried to resist. I tried really hard to turn

round and hurry back to the house, but the call of the line was too strong. I know now that I was mesmerized by its straightness and sparkle.

I walked out to the middle of the spotless new road, and put one blue foot on the line. Nothing bad happened, so I put the other foot in front of the first one. Heel to toe. That was the proper way to walk a line.

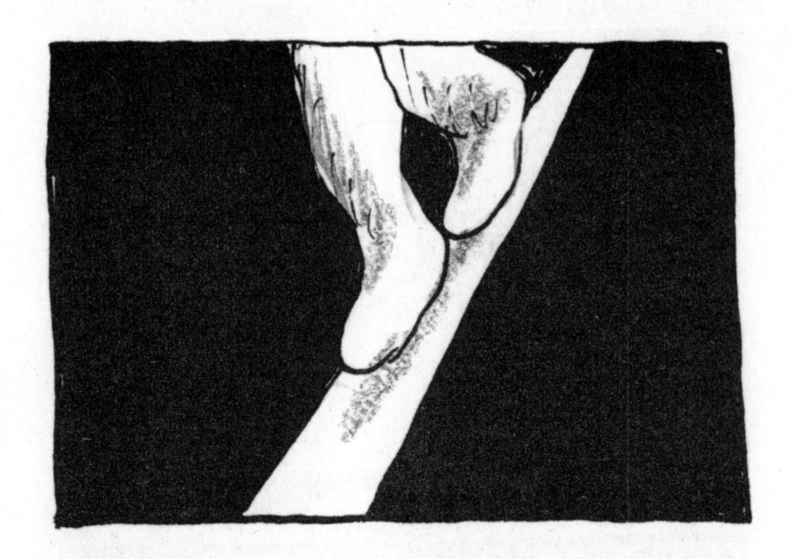

Marty was delighted. 'See! Now, just keep walking the line. On and on and on, forever. If you come to a house with people in it and dogs and a canary and stuff, then you can live with them and eat *their* jumbo jelly babies.'

I didn't hear anything after the first bit.

Now, just keep walking the line. On and on and on, forever.

I took one baby step, then another. Everything else left my tiny baby brain, except the wish that I could walk this line forever. It really was the best line in the world, because you could feel it as well as see it. It pushed up out of the road like a fat stripe of plasticine. I forgot about my mum and dad, I forgot about my brothers and jelly babies. The only thing in my head was this wonderful line.

'Bye bye, Will,' called Marty. 'I hope you find a nice house, far, far away.'

'Bye bye, Mary,' I replied, and set off down the wonderful line.

It worked, thought Marty, squeezing under the fence and racing home, hopefully before Mum realized that he was gone. Marty could really run when he was in a hurry, and he timed himself from the fence. He was never a great counter, so Marty timed himself by singing 'Little Drummer Boy' and seeing how far he got. It only took him as far as 'I am a poor boy too, pa rum pum pum pum' to reach the back door.

Meanwhile, I was happily walking the line. I really was an excellent line walker, and my feet hardly ever landed on the tarmacadam. Which was just as well, because the fresh tar was still wet and sticky in spots, and whenever I touched the road, a black rubbery string stuck to my foot and stretched out behind me like a trail of chewing gum. But even these rubbery ropes tugging at my feet could not ruin my enjoyment of this wonderful line.

On and on I went, heel to toe. After a while, I came to a gentle bend in the road. I was a bit disappointed by this; a line going around a bend cannot really be a straight line. But I decided to forgive it and keep walking. After all it did straighten out again after the turn. In fact, by the time it reached the orange traffic cones, where the new road joined the old road and where all the traffic was, the line was as straight as an arrow.

CHAPTER 6

A Handful of Ears

Marty sneaked back into the house, and tried to look relaxed and innocent. When Dad was relaxing, he put his feet up on the sofa and read the newspaper. So Marty pulled the local paper from the table and spread it over himself on the sofa. The newspaper was so big that Marty looked like he was in another makeshift tent. In fact, when Mum came out of the kitchen, and saw Marty's head sticking out from underneath the paper, she thought that he was playing camping.

'That's another nice tent, Marty,' she said, tickling under Marty's chin.

'Sorry, Mum,' said Marty. 'Can't talk. Reading important news stuff.'

'I see,' said Mum seriously. 'There's a lot of important news stuff happening in town this week.' She tapped an article on the front page. 'They're opening the new road soon. It's going to get a lot noisier around here, and more dangerous with all the cars and trucks. We're going to have to be extra careful from now on.'

Marty didn't like the sound of being extra careful. He had just put his little brother on the new road.

'Cahs and twucks?' he said nervously. When Marty got nervous, he had trouble saying his Rs.

'Oh yes. That new road will be the main route to Dublin. All the trucks from the ferry

will use it. Dad is putting a stronger catch on the gate to make sure Will stays away from the cars. You know what a little monkey he is. Even now, all that separates the new road from the old one is a bunch of traffic cones. The last place any child should be is near that new road.'

Marty went paler than the bits of newspaper without any writing on them.

'What's the matter, Marty?' asked Mum, who knew Marty's guilty face when she saw it.

Marty didn't say anything. He didn't want me to get hurt, but he didn't want to get into trouble either, and for all he knew I had already moved in with another family.

'Marty! What have you done?'

Mum searched the room for me. Usually when Marty had done something wrong, I was on the receiving end.

'Where's Will, Marty? Where's your little brother?' Then Mum realized what she and Marty had just been talking about.

'Oh no. You put him on the road, didn't you?'

To Marty, this deduction seemed like a feat of magic. He didn't know that mothers can tell most of what is going on in their children's heads just by looking at their faces.

'Yes,' he wailed. 'I didn't know about the cahs and twucks. I'm sowwy.'

Mum ran into the kitchen. 'Will's on the new

road,' she said to my gran. 'Keep an eye on the boys, would you? And make sure that Marty doesn't set foot off that sofa. We're going to have a serious talk when I get back.'

Marty hid his face under the newspaper. However bad he felt at that moment, he suspected that he would shortly be feeling a lot worse.

I was making my way slowly towards the orange traffic cones. To be honest, I was getting a little tired of walking, and the tar strings were making each step a struggle. The noise of the traffic from the old road was growing louder now, and I could see swirling dust clouds where the trucks thundered past. Of course at age two, I wasn't thinking words like *swirling* or *dust clouds*. I was probably thinking something like: *Will tired. Will want Mummy.*

And, as if my wish had been granted, I heard Mum's voice behind me. I looked round, and there she was, vaulting the fence, then running down the centre of the road towards me. She was waving her hands and shouting. Of course *now* I know that she wanted me to stop where I was, but at the time I thought we were having a game of chase.

I always liked a good game of chase, so I ran as fast as my tar-soaked boots would allow, straight for the orange cones. They must be the winning point.

Mum screamed louder, so I ran faster. This was fun.

'Fun,' I squeaked. 'Will run! Mummy can't catch.'

But Mummy could catch; she was an ex-infant teacher and used to running after fleeing children. She put her head down and sprinted, determined to nab me before I reached the old road and the thundering traffic.

With several long strides she caught up with me, seconds before I reached the cones. She reached out and grabbed my blue bunny ears, hoisting me into the air.

'Oh, thank goodness,' she gasped, holding the ears tightly. 'That was a close one.'

When Mum's breathing slowed down a bit she noticed that my bunny suit felt a bit light. This was because I wasn't in it. I was still toddling towards the cones, dressed only in boots and cloth nappy. When Mum had grabbed the bunny ears and yanked, she had popped all the clips on my jumpsuit, allowing me to slip out of the leg holes.

'Aaaaahhh!' screamed Mum. 'I don't believe this.'

But she did believe it, because it was happening. I had reached the cones and passed straight through to the old road. There I stood, doing a victory bounce, with traffic coming from both sides.

So, in desperation, Mum did something that mums are not supposed to do. She told a lie. Sort of.

'Look, Will,' she said, holding out an empty closed fist. Then she sang, 'Who's the best boy in the world?'

'I am! I am!' I squealed, and ran to claim my prize.

'Yes, you are,' said Mum, gathering me

into her arms. 'And you're the worst boy in the world too for giving me a fright like that.' Then Mum hugged me so tightly that I completely forgot about the jumbo jelly baby that I should have won.

She kept me wrapped in her embrace until we were back inside the garden gate, far away from the dangerous traffic.

When we got home, everyone was in big trouble, even Dad.

'You were supposed to put a stronger catch on that gate!' said Mum.

'I'm going to do it now,' said Dad, hurrying out with his toolbox. 'Right now.'

I was next. 'And what were you doing going out on the road? That is the most dangerous place in the world. Even a two-year-old knows that.'

'Sorry, Mum,' I mumbled, then remembered

the prize that I was supposed to have won out on the road. 'Jumbo jelly baby?'

Mum's face went bright red. 'Jelly baby? Now he wants a jelly baby. You're lucky that I don't lock you in the playpen for a year. Now go and put your boots in the bin. They're completely ruined.'

Even at two, I knew that this was not the time to argue about the jelly baby.

Marty was still under the newspaper. It crackled like leaves in the wind as he shivered with nervousness.

'Come out from under there, Master Martin Woodman,' said Mum. When Mum is really angry, she calls us all by our full names and adds a *Master* at the beginning.

'Did you open the gate and let Will on to the new road?'

Marty pretended he was reading the paper. 'Sowwy, Mum. Weading news stuff.'

Mum snatched away the paper.

'Never mind the news stuff; we have our own breaking story right here.'

Marty knew he was in the worst trouble of his life. It's not easy for a four-year-old to get into trouble – they can be forgiven almost anything just by wobbling their lips – you have to do something *really* bad.

'Don't even bother with the lip thing,' warned Mum. 'I am too cross for that.'

Marty decided to try the oldest trick in the book. He spoke slowly, concentrating.

'I love you, Mummy. And Daddy and Will and my little baby brother, I forget his name. But I love him too.'

Mum was not impressed. 'I love you too, Marty, but this time you have gone too far, even for a four-year-old. This is the worst thing you have ever done, so you will receive the worst punishment I have ever handed out.'

I came back into the room, just in time to hear what this punishment would be.

'For two weeks, you will row the bath every evening after tea.'

Rowing the bath does not sound like a serious punishment – certainly not serious enough to have Marty howling on the sofa and stamping his heels on the cushions as he was. But rowing the bath is more serious than it sounds. In most homes, babies wear disposable nappies that get thrown out when they are used. Not in our house. Mum and Dad are determined to do their part to clean up the environment, and so they use cloth nappies. *Reusable nappies*.

This means that in those days, two boys' worth of stinky nappies had to be washed. That amount of nappies would clog up a washing machine, so Dad developed his own washing method. The nappies were dumped into a plastic baby bath, soaked in hot water and washing powder, and stirred with a canoe paddle cut in half. This method was known as rowing the nappies. No child had ever been forced to row the nappies before, but over the years it would become a popular and effective punishment. Popular with our parents, effective with the kids.

Obviously the more used the nappies were, the less fun they were to stir. Some days were worse than others. It depended on what we had been eating. Vegetables, for example, were good for our health, but bad for our nappies.

And as Marty lay there on the sofa, thrashing in despair, Donnie looked on from the playpen with a little grin on his baby face. It was almost as if he knew that Marty was in trouble, and all he had to do to make things worse for him was eat his vegetables.

For the next two weeks, Mum was amazed to find that all her children gobbled down their carrots and peas at dinnertime. We couldn't get enough of them. All except Marty.

CHAPTER 7

Peg Leg's Spiral Staircase

So this was the story I told Grandad the following Saturday in the lighthouse. The story of how Marty had abandoned me on the new road.

I enjoyed telling it. It was a fabulous story, and it would be difficult to beat.

When I had finished, I knew Grandad was impressed. He had stopped polishing the lenses halfway through and stood there with his mouth open.

'Are you sure this is all true?' he asked.

'Yes. Dad told me.'

'It's just that there are a lot of details there. Things that your dad wouldn't have known.'

'I checked details with Mum and Gran. Even Marty remembers bits.'

Grandad poured some polish on to his rag. 'Well, that's a good one, Bosun. Left out on the road. Yours is a sad and troubled past.'

I grinned from ear to ear, delighted to hear it. I only hoped that I could find another miserable story for next week.

'That Marty is quite a scamp,' added Grandad.

I was surprised to hear myself sticking up for Marty. 'He's not so bad. He was only four at the time.'

'He hasn't changed much though, has he?'

'I suppose not,' I said, thinking of Tuesday morning when Marty had covered a tennis ball with tinfoil and convinced me that he had

found a priceless moon rock.

'You win this week, Bosun,' said Grandad. 'I don't have anything to top that.'

'Being bitten on the head by a shark is pretty good too, Grandad,' I said generously.

Grandad ruffled my hair with his free hand. 'I thought so too, until I heard your story.'

After we had finished polishing, we climbed the 116 steps back down to the ground floor.

Grandad stopped on the first step, the big one, and sat on it. He patted it for me to sit beside him. Which I did.

'You know something, Will. Seeing as you're my little Bosun, I should really tell you the legend of Peg Leg's spiral staircase . . .'

'I know that one,' I interrupted. 'You told me already. Peg Leg couldn't manage the high steps so he carved them down over the years, but he died before finishing the last one.'

Grandad winked. 'Ah, that's the official story. That's what we tell tourists. Only the lighthouse keepers and their Bosuns know the real story, and I think it's time I passed on the story to you. Do you want to hear it?'

I nodded. What nine-year-old would not be interested in hearing a secret story?

Grandad leaned in close, in case anyone might overhear. 'The truth is that old Peg Leg had no problem climbing the steps; in fact, he had a special short wooden leg that helped him around the bends.'

'So why did he carve down the steps?' I whispered.

'He didn't,' said Grandad. 'Peg Leg got so fed up of his father-in-law complaining about the steep steps that he built up the first one.'

'Why would he do that?' I wondered aloud.

'So when his father-in-law visited the following year, Peg Leg could tell him that he had carved down all the steps just for him, except the first one which he hadn't got around to yet.'

'Didn't his father-in-law notice?'

'No,' cackled Grandad. 'The first step is so high that all the others seem small. His father-in-law thanked him and judged him the best son-in-law a man could have. He even left Peg Leg a thousand pounds in his will, and never complained about the steps again. In fact, nobody ever complains about the steps, because the big one makes the rest seem small.'

Grandad winked at me. 'There's a moral for you in that story, you know. In fact, it's a bit like our Saturday complaining sessions.'

'What's the moral in the story?'

Grandad stood. 'You need to work that out for yourself.'

I frowned. 'No, Grandad, I mean what is a *moral*? What am I supposed to figure out for myself?'

'A moral,' said Grandad. 'Is a secret message inside the story.'

'Like a spy code?'

Grandad swatted me with one of his rags. 'No. Not like a spy code. More like a second hidden story.'

'Like invisible ink?'

'No, Bosun,' said Grandad, pretending to strangle me. 'It's like the story itself paints a picture that's not in the words.'

'Like hieroglyphics?'

Grandad made a face. 'Are you sure you're my grandson, dopey? I give up. Ask your mother, she's the teacher in the family.'

So I asked Mum on the way home in the car.

'Mum, what's the moral of a story?'

And Mum said, 'Bert, stop picking your nose.' And then, 'Donnie, don't adjust the mirror to look at yourself.' And, 'HP, get your hand out of your brother's sock.' And finally, 'The moral of a story is the lesson that the story teaches us.'

'For example?' I said. With Mum there was always a *for example*.

'For example "The Hare and the Tortoise". The moral of that story is that sometimes it's better to do something slowly and carefully than rush through it.'

I thought about that for a while. What was the moral of Peg Leg's spiral staircase? Grandad had said that the big step made all the others seem small. What did that have to do with our Saturday sessions? All we did was talk about our problems, and Grandad's had always been bigger than mine. Until today.

Suddenly I understood, because I am extremely bright, as it says on my report card in the comments section. Our problems were like Peg Leg's steps. And Grandad's big

problems always made my problems seem smaller. Grandad had been making me feel better, without me even knowing about it. Until today. Maybe today I made Grandad feel better.

I smiled, and Mum saw me in the rear-view mirror.

'You look pleased with yourself, Will. Do you know what the moral of a story is now?'

'Yes,' I replied. 'I do.'

Puffin by Post

The Legend of the Worst Boy in the World – Eoin Colfer

If you have enjoyed this book and want to read more,
then check out these other great Puffin titles.
You can order any of the following books direct with Puffin by Post:

The Legend of Spud Murphy • Eoin Colfer • 9780141317083	£4.99
'The funniest book of the year . . . a mini masterpiece' – *Daily Mail*	

The Legend of Captain Crow's Teeth • Eoin Colfer • 9780141318905	£4.99
'Family capers and full-on belly laughs' – *Funday Times*	

My Brother's Famous Bottom • Jeremy Strong • 9780141322384	£4.99
'Jeremy Strong is the King of Comedy' – *Guardian*	

Spy Dog • Andrew Cope • 9780141318844	£4.99
'We love Lara!' – *Kraze Club*	

The Jenius • Dick King-Smith • 9780141312866	£4.99
'Dick King-Smith knows what children like' – *Guardian*	

Just contact:

Puffin Books, C/o Bookpost, PO Box 29,
Douglas, Isle of Man, IM99 1BQ
Credit cards accepted. For further details:
Telephone: 01624 677237
Fax: 01624 670923

You can email your orders to: bookshop@enterprise.net
Or order online at: www.bookpost.co.uk

Free delivery in the UK.
Overseas customers must add £2 per book.

Prices and availability are subject to change.

Visit puffin.co.uk to find out about the latest titles, read extracts and exclusive author interviews, and enter exciting competitions.
You can also browse thousands of Puffin books online.